THE HOUSE BOOK

by Carol North
illustrated by Ellen Dolce

A GOLDEN BOOK • NEW YORK

Western Publishing Company, Inc., Racine, Wisconsin 53404

Josh's house is the third house
on the block. It has a big front yard
and red shutters on the windows.

Josh comes home from school. He climbs the
porch steps and goes inside his house.

In the front hall, Josh hangs his jacket in the closet.

Grandma is talking with a friend in the living room. Josh waves hello.

Mother is cooking dinner in the kitchen. Josh has a snack at the counter.

In the back yard, Josh plays basketball for a while.

Then Josh goes into the garage. Daddy is fixing the lawn mower. Josh helps him.

It's time for dinner. The table is set in the dining room. Josh is hungry tonight!

After dinner, everyone relaxes in the family room. Josh plays a game with Grandma.

Soon it's time for Josh's bath. The bathroom is upstairs.

After his bath, Josh puts on his pajamas and goes into his bedroom. He climbs into bed with his teddy bear and his baseball glove.

Good night, Josh!

This is Josh's house.